Junebug
and the Gumbo Garden

Story by

Tameka Bradley Hobbs

Illustrated by

Jason Austin

D1115974

For Ashanti and Amiri

CHAPTER 1

The sun had just come up on what was bound to be the absolute hottest day in July in Johnsonville, Mississippi. The sounds of moving trucks interrupted the sleepy peace of the quiet neighborhood. The Jones family was moving from the Windy City itself—Chicago, Illinois—into their new home on Juniper Street. They were a quaint family of three: Gregory Cornelius Jones, better known as Greg; his wife, Gina; and their son, Gregory Cornelius Jones, Junior, affectionately known to his family as Junebug. And, last but not least, their dog Jack-Jack.

As soon as the cab of the truck opened, Junebug darted out and started down the sidewalk, Jack-Jack galloping behind. They had been on the road too long and were tired of being cooped up in the truck.

"Get back here, Junebug!" yelled Greg.

"Aww, Dad, I just want to stretch my legs," Junebug whined.

"Just look at our new house!" Gina exclaimed as she grabbed Greg's hand and Junebug's shoulder. The three of them stood on the sidewalk and stared at the

house at 627 Juniper Street. It was gray with light green
shutters and three gables on the top. "That's the
window in your room," Gina said to Junebug, pointing
to the gable on the right side of the house.

"Cool!" exclaimed Junebug.

"And the sooner we get the truck unloaded, the
sooner you can enjoy it," said Greg, stretching his back.

"O.K. What can I do?" asked Junebug. A few hours later, he regretted asking that question. Helping unload the truck was hard work. There seemed to be hundreds of boxes that weighed hundreds of pounds. Junebug lifted and pushed and pushed and tugged and tugged and lifted. His arms and back began to ache. "Mom, I'm thirsty. Can we take a break?"

Gina joined Junebug on the porch, wiping the sweat from her forehead. "That's a great idea." She strolled to the truck and grabbed some bottled water from the cooler. She tossed a bottle to Greg as he came out of the house and let the screen door slam behind him. She met Junebug on the front steps and had a seat, passing him his bottle. He frowned at it but remembered that they drank all the grape sodas during their trip. He looked up and saw Jack-Jack, playfully rolling around in the grass with his tongue hanging out of his mouth. Junebug frowned again. *Lucky dog*, he thought to himself. *He doesn't have to do any work.* Before they could crack their bottles open, they heard a faint voice calling.

"Hey, chile!"

It was coming from the yard next to theirs.

"Hey, chile!" the voice said again. "Over here! Ya'll look like you could use somethin' taste better than some plain ol' water, hard as ya'll been workin'."

They looked over in the direction of the voice. It was coming from a woman standing at the low white picket fence in the yard of the house next door. She was an old lady in a blue flowered dress with a cane. She had a head full of thick, gray hair that she wore in two braids which fell over her shoulders.

Junebug followed as his mom and dad stepped down off the porch and headed over to the fence. As they got closer, they could see that beside the old woman was a cart that held a pitcher of icy lemonade, glasses, and a plate full of what looked like cookies.

"Good to meet ya! Good to meet ya! My name is Marguerite Gautier and this is my house. So I guess that makes us somethin' like neighbors."

Greg and Gina smiled widely and extended their hands. "My name is Greg Jones. This is my wife Gina and my son, Greg, Jr."

"Everyone calls me Junebug," he said.

"Why hello there, lil' fella! What a fine young man you are!" Looking him up and down, Miss Gautier extended her hand across the fence, reaching for Junebug's hand. He didn't want to be rude so he approached the fence to meet her grasp. Her hands were wrinkled and soft but her grip was firm. She looked the same age as his Grandma Pearl, but Grandma Pearl didn't have a grip like that. As he got closer, Junebug noticed that Miss Gautier smelled like flowers, pepper, and ointment mixed together. He gazed over her silver-rimmed glasses and into her eyes, which were the strangest shade of gray he'd ever seen. Seeing her made him miss his Grandma Pearl even more.

Just then Jack-Jack came running up. "And Miss Gautier," said Junebug, "this is my dog, Jack-Jack. Say hello, Jack-Jack. Shake her hand." Junebug had worked all summer to teach Jack-Jack to shake hands. As he came closer to the fence, instead of sitting down like he normally did to shake hands, Jack-Jack began to act strangely. He stood up on all four legs and sniffed suspiciously around Miss Gautier. All of a sudden, his ears lay back on his head and he began to bark loudly at her.

"Jack-Jack! Down, Jack-Jack!" said Greg. "I'm sorry, Miss Gautier. I don't know what's gotten into him."

"Oh, honey, that's alright. Who knows why dogs do like they do? That good ol' doggy nose of his might just smell Toussaint on me."

"Toussaint? Who's that?" asked Junebug.

Just then he heard a soft, low meowing from beneath Miss Gautier's skirt. As he looked down, Junebug saw a cat, all black with bright, glowing green eyes, walk forward, wrapping his tail around Miss Gautier's ankles.

"This here is Toussaint, baby, my very best friend. He's an absolute rascal, so watch out for him," she said while grinning broadly. "Enough about that crazy cat. Have some of this here lemonade before all the ice melts."

"And what about the cookies? Are those for us, too?" exclaimed Junebug, gazing greedily at her cart.

"Greg, Jr., where are your manners?" Gina chided.

"Oh, that's alright. A growing boy's s'posed to have a big appetite and big eyes for sweets, too. But those are not cookies, chile. Those what you call teacakes. Kind of an old-fashioned cookie made with molasses. Just like my grandmama used to bake for me. And you can have all you like, if it's alright with ya mama and daddy."

"Mom, can I?" he asked eagerly.

"Alright. Go ahead. What do you say to the nice lady?"

"Thank you, Miss Gautier!" *If I'm getting lemonade and cookies on the first day,* Junebug thought to himself, *I just might like living here.*

Gina and Greg continued to talk to Miss Gautier while they sipped their lemonade. "I must say—those are some beautiful flowers on your porch," said Gina.

"Why thank you for noticing. If you think this is somethin', you should have seen my garden back home in Nawleans, chile, back at my family's place, 'fore Trina ran us all outta dere. After the storm, I came here and started again. I do what I can when ol' Arthur lets me. I let most of my flowers go, 'cept for my prize rosebush. Mama used to say 'a garden without a rosebush is like gumbo without okra' and I believe she was right!" Miss Gautier chuckled.

After they had enjoyed their snacks and said their thank-you's, the Joneses went back into their new home to finish unpacking. "She seems like such a sweet lady," said Gina. "That's a shame about the storm."

"Mama, who is Trina and why did she make Miss Gautier leave her house? And what is *Nawleans?*" asked Junebug.

Greg and Gina exchanged looks and muffled laughs. "When she said 'Trina,' it was short for Katrina," replied Gina. "You remember, right? That big hurricane a couple of years ago?"

"Junie," added Greg, "you remember we watched the news together when those people left their homes and had to stay in the Superdome? That was in New Orleans, but people from that way pronounce it *Nawleans.* That's what Miss Gautier was saying."

"Oh, yeah, Dad, I remember. We talked about that at school, and collected clothes and food to send to the victims," Junebug chimed. "Miss Gautier was there?"

"Yes, looks like it. She and a lot of other people lost their homes and had to start all over again," answered Greg.

"I wonder if she lives there all alone," said Gina.

"It looks like that might be the case. She seems so eager to make new friends, with the lemonade and all. She's probably a little lonely," said Greg. "We'll just have to make a point to look out for her. Good neighbors look out for each other."

"Yeah, we need to do that," said Junebug as they walked up the steps to their new house. "She talks funny but she sure does make some good cookies."

"You and your belly, boy!" laughed Greg. Gina giggled and shook her head.

CHAPTER 2

At first Junebug hated the idea of moving. When they first found out about it, his mom and dad were excited because of his dad's new job at the automobile plant. Gina was *really* excited about finding a new house. After all the arrangements were final, everything began to change. It was hard for Junebug to say goodbye to his old house. It was the only one he had ever lived in. Junebug watched as what seemed like every little bit of his life was packed away into cardboard boxes. He had to box up his rock collection, along with all of his favorite storybooks. Then he had to put away his baseballs, bats, his glove, his computer, water guns, colored pencils, soccer ball, and basketball. All around the house it was the same story. Before long, Junebug didn't even have anywhere to sit. On top of everything else, Junebug was sad because he was leaving all of his friends—Freddie, Antwan, Malek, and Taylor. He would miss their ball games and sleepovers. He'd have to make new friends, which was a scary thought to Junebug. Besides, who wanted to move to Mississippi anyway?

After everything was packed, the family went to live with Grandma Pearl while the men loaded the boxes into the moving truck. On the morning they left, Grandma Pearl gave him a big hug, kissed him on his forehead, and gave him a huge chunk of her special pound cake to eat during the trip. Then Greg, Gina, and Junebug began the long drive to Johnsonville. It seemed like the truck would never stop.

After they arrived at the new house, it was the same thing all over again: more boxes. Junebug didn't think they would ever get their things unpacked. What was worse, Junebug hardly ever got to go outside and have fun. His mom always had something for him to do. "Junebug, would you bag up all of this newspaper and take it to the curb?" "Junebug, could you be a dear and break down these boxes?" He thought it would never end.

Before long, the mountains of boxes began to disappear. Soon the new house was starting to look like home. Before he knew it, it was time to go to school. Junebug would be attending Johnsonville Elementary. It was only a few blocks away so he would be able to walk to and from school on his own. That was cool because it was something he could do by himself.

Junebug was very excited about his first day at his new school. Many thoughts raced through his mind. He hoped that he would like his new teacher. He also hoped that he would make some new friends. As he came around the corner Junebug could see his new school building. It wasn't a cool building like his old school in Chicago; instead it was an old-looking brick building. It even had a bell on top like some he'd seen in storybooks. He was assigned to Mrs. Gerber's fourth grade class. She seemed really cool. All of the other kids were nice to him and after he introduced himself to the class, they had questions about where he'd come from. They asked him if he'd ever been to the Sears Tower, and about snow, since, as Junebug learned, it hardly ever snowed in Mississippi.

After talking to some of the other students, Junebug discovered that there were a bunch of kids who lived in the neighborhood and they walked to and from school together. He saw them leaving for home after school and he ran to catch up.

"Wait up, you guys!" he yelled, running behind the group. "You guys live near Juniper Street, right?" he panted once he was within earshot.

"Yeah," said one of the boys.

"Me, too. Mind if I walk with you?"

"No problem," said the girl in the group.

"I just moved here. My name is Greg, but everybody calls me Junebug."

"Junebug?! What kind of name is that?" said one of the boys, but the girl gave him a hard elbow in the arm and frowned at him.

"Hi. I'm Kareem."

"My name is Larry."

"What's up, Greg, I mean Junebug? My name is Jennifer, but everyone calls me Jenny. So where did you move from?"

"I used to live in Chicago but my dad got a new job so we moved here," said Junebug, wiping sweat from his forehead. "Where do you live?"

"My house is on the corner of Juniper and Cypress Street. Kareem lives next door to me."

"I live a little bit farther up the block on Oak Street," said Larry. "It's right next to the playground."

"How 'bout you?" asked Kareem. "Where you live?"

"We live at 627 Juniper Street."

"Is that the gray house?" Kareem asked with concern in his voice. They all stopped and spun around to look at Junebug, waiting for his answer.

"Well, yeah, it is gray," Junebug replied cautiously as he tried to read their faces. "Why?"

"Have you met the witch yet?" asked Larry.

"Witch?" Junebug asked, confused. "What witch?"

"You don't know that. You need to stop saying that," said Kareem to Larry.

"Who are you talking about?" said Junebug.

"He means Marguerite Gautier," said Jenny. "They say she's a straight-up witch. An ol' creole hoo-doo lady from Louisiana."

"You mean Miss Gautier?" asked Junebug.

"Yep, that's her. You met her already?" asked Jenny.

"You didn't eat anything she made, did you?" Larry asked, grabbing Junebug's shoulder in a serious manner.

"Well, yeah. She gave my mom, my dad, and I some cookies and lemonade one day. What's hoo-doo?" Junebug said nervously. *People talk weird here*, he thought to himself, looking at Jenny.

"Oh, man, she got you now!" exclaimed Jenny.

"W-w-what do you mean?" Junebug was becoming alarmed.

"Hey man," Kareem grabbed him by the wrist and pulled him down the sidewalk. "Don't let these two fill your head with all that stuff."

"Word to the wise, man: never eat anything a hoo-doo witch gives you," said Larry.

"Now she has you under her spell," said Jenny in her best creepy voice, as she stretched her eyes and wiggled her fingers towards Junebug.

"Spell? She's a witch?!! WHAT IS HOO-DOO?" Junebug stopped in his tracks, waving his hands in the air out of frustration.

"Hoo-doo is evil magic that comes from Louisiana and that's where Miss Gautier's from," whispered Jenny.

"Yeah. She can turn you into a zombie and make you do her bidding," said Larry, jabbing Jenny in the arm with his elbow.

"You guys are trippin'. Don't pay them any attention, man," urged Kareem.

Junebug didn't believe what he was hearing. Miss Gautier was a nice lady who had to leave her home because of Hurricane Katrina. She couldn't be what Larry and Jenny said she was. "O.K., so if she is a witch, how do you know?"

"I got two words for you: Dennis Muldrow," said Jenny.

"Who is that?"

"He ended up being one of Miss Gautier's victims," said Larry.

"What do you mean?"

"Poor little ol' Dennis used to live across the street from where you live now. He went to school with us, too. He would always tell us about how nice Miss Gautier was to him. He would go over to see her almost every day. He went over so much that he stopped coming to the park to hang out with us. Next thing you know, there's no sign of Dennis anywhere. He just – POOF! – disappeared," Jenny said, clapping her hands together for emphasis.

"We haven't seen him since," added Larry.

"So what happened to him?"

"All that hanging out with the witch. She finally got him," replied Jenny.

"And Missy Fulton from over on Sycamore Street. Her house was right behind Miss Gautier's," said Larry.

"That's right! I almost forgot," Jenny chimed. "And Johnny Lightfoot. Remember him?"

"Yeap," said Larry, snapping his fingers.

"And Sidney Pullam. And Veronica Mitchell."

"Yeah, man," said Larry. "You better watch your back."

"That's not all. I heard that those hoo-doo women eat children so they can stay strong and young looking. You know, like she's trying to live forever," said Jenny, whispering and looking over her shoulder like someone was there listening to her.

Kareem rolled his eyes. "So now she's graduated from witch to vampire. Make up your mind which story you're going with, Jen."

"Hey, I'm just trying to save your boy's life here. What's your name again, homie?"

"You can call me Greg," he said, remembering their earlier reaction to his nickname.

"Yeah, Greg. I'm just trying to keep you from ending up like Dennis. If you don't want to listen, that's on you."

The group reached the corner and Junebug turned to go home. "Well, thanks anyway for the warning. Do you guys walk to school in the morning?"

"Yeah."

"Tomorrow morning wait for me here and I'll walk with you."

"O.K. See you then," said Kareem.

"*Maybe* we'll see you," snickered Larry as he crossed the street.

"That's not funny, Larry," said Jenny as she walked behind him. "See you tomorrow, Greg."

Junebug watched them as they crossed the street and turned to walk home. He didn't know what to think about what Larry and Jenny said about Miss Gautier. He didn't believe witches were real. Yeah, he'd read about them in ghost stories, but a real live witch in the house next door to him? That was just too unreal. Besides, Miss Gautier was just a nice old lady. He didn't get any witchy vibes at all from her.

There was another explanation, too. Maybe Larry and Jenny were just making up the story to scare him because he was the new kid on the block. They could be playing a joke on him behind his back. Well, no one was going to make a fool out of Gregory Cornelius Jones, Junior! If he was living next door to a witch, he would know. Besides, Miss Gautier was too nice, and her cookies were too good, for her to be a witch.

CHAPTER 3

Aside from his new friends' rumors about Miss Gautier, Junebug's first week of school was pretty uneventful. Because they walked to and from school together just about every day, Jenny, Kareem, and Larry became his closest friends. Jenny and Larry still tried to convince Junebug that their stories about Miss Gautier being a witch were true, but more and more they talked about other things like events at school and comics, and made their own fun.

One Friday the gang invited him to play with them on Saturday at the community park next to Larry's house. Junebug jumped at the chance. If he didn't have any plans his mom and dad would surely give him chores around the house, since they still had so much unpacking to do. *Why should I spend my free day in the house when I could be out having fun?*, Junebug thought to himself.

The next day, after eating a couple of bowls of Mighty Crunchy Puffs and watching "Captain Kung Pow," his favorite cartoon, Junebug made his way to the community park. Larry was already there when he arrived, and before long Kareem and Jenny showed up. They started off on the monkey bars, trading tricks, and having a competition to see who could hang upside down the longest. Then they competed to see who could hang by their arms the longest. Junebug couldn't hang for very long. The other kids teased him because his shirt kept rising up over his big round stomach.

After they finished on the playground, the gang decided to play a game of kickball. Two kids he didn't know were chosen as captains. Once they started picking teams, Junebug was picked last. He wasn't surprised because back at his old school in Chicago the same thing happened. The kids assumed that because he was a little heavy that he was slow. Now, Junebug wasn't the fastest runner but he was good at kickball. He had strong legs and would kick the ball so far that he usually made it to third base or to home base before anyone in the outfield could even make it back within throwing distance. Sure enough, Junebug made the other team regret they didn't pick him, especially after he earned seven points for his team.

By the afternoon, Junebug and the other children began to head home. After a day of playing, Junebug could feel his stomach beginning to rumble. His mouth watered when he thought about the sandwiches his mother probably had waiting on him. That's usually what she made for lunch on Saturdays. As he approached his house, Junebug saw his mother sitting on Miss Gautier's porch, talking to the old lady. As he got closer he heard them sharing a laugh.

"Junebug, come here," Gina called out to him. "Come speak to Miss Gautier." She raised a glass of lemonade to her lips.

"Hello, Miss Gautier. How are you today?"

"Why, just fine, baby, just fine. Thanks for asking. You look like you could use a drink. You been playing hard?"

"Yes ma'am. I was playing kickball down at the

park."

"Here. Have a glass of this lemonade. I just brought some out here for ya mama." She poured some of the pale yellow liquid from a pitcher into a mason jar she had sitting on a tray.

"What do you say, son?" Gina gave him a look that said, *Where are your manners?*

"Thank you."

"Well, you surely are welcome. Any time." Miss Gautier gazed sweetly at him with her gray eyes twinkling over her glasses.

"Junebug, you are right on time. Miss Gautier and I were just discussing how you might be able to help her out."

"That's right, young man. As much as I want to, I can't get 'round in this here yard like I want to. That ol' Arthur keeps me down somethin' terrible." Leaning on her cane, Miss Gautier reached down and rubbed her knee.

"Well, why don't you tell him to get off of you so you can work?," asked Junebug.

Gina and Miss Gautier looked at each other and snickered. "No baby, she means her arthritis. 'Arthur' is short for arthritis."

"Oh," said Junebug, a bit embarrassed.

"I was thinking that maybe you could help Miss Gautier work in her yard after school a few days each week."

"That would be a big help. Now, Miss Gautier don't have a lot of money, but I could cook up somethin' good for you to eat every now and then to trade for your work. How that sound to you, baby?" Miss Gautier asked.

"Well, Junebug, what do you say?" Gina asked. By

the look in her eye, Junebug knew that he really didn't
have a choice.

"Yes ma'am, I'll help you."

"Oh, bless you, baby," Miss Gautier exclaimed as she
jostled his chin with her soft knuckles. She smelled like
ointment and mothballs. As Junebug looked into her
face he noticed a curious gleam in her eye. "You just
don't know what a big help you'll be."

CHAPTER 4

On Monday, Junebug made a point not to mention to any of his friends that he would be working for Miss Gautier. He didn't want to take the heat from them. So they walked home just like normal after school. As they approached the corner where they usually went their separate ways, Kareem grabbed Junebug by the shoulder. "Hey, can you come down to the park a little later? Some of the kids from the neighborhood want a kickball rematch. You really helped us kick their butts on Saturday and we could use your help again today. Can you come out?"

"Well – ummm …" stuttered Junebug.

"Yeah, man, you got some skills. Can you come play on our team?" Larry chimed in.

"Well – ummm – I think my mom said something about, something about us going – ummm – oh yeah, she wants me to go to the store with her after school today. So I probably won't be able to make it."

"That's too bad," said Jenny. "What do you have to get from the store anyway?"

"Who knows," Junebug laughed nervously. "You know how parents are. You guys have fun without me. I'll see you tomorrow."

"Alright, man. Later," said Kareem as he and the others crossed the street.

That was close, Junebug thought to himself. He didn't like being dishonest with his friends but what other choice did he have? He didn't want to let his mother down and he didn't want to have his friends joning on him for working with Miss Gautier. Lying just seemed like the easiest thing to do.

As Junebug got closer to his house, he saw that Miss Gautier was already in her yard. She had on a big straw hat with a purple sash around the top that tied under her chin. As she bent over her two gray braids flopped on top of her shoulders. She wore a big green dress with flowers all over it. As she walked around, she leaned on her cane with her left hand and in her right hand she carried a watering can, from which she rained liquid on the plants growing around her porch.

"Come on over here, boy. Just drop your things on the porch," she called to Junebug when she saw him walking towards the house. He opened the gate and began to walk towards her house. As he looked around at her yard, Junebug almost regretted agreeing so easily to work with her. Miss Gautier's entire front yard was a humongous tangle of green. There seemed to be as many thorns as there were flowers. Everything was overgrown, reaching as high as his thigh, and in other places as high as his waist. "Before we get going, I made a lil' somethin' for you." She put down her pail and ushered Junebug over to a tray resting in the corner of the porch. On it sat a sandwich, another one of those big cookies, and an icy glass of lemonade. "You a growing boy and you gon need ya energy for all the work we have to do. That's somethin' called a po' boy sandwich they eat down in Nawleans."

She must have read my mind, Junebug said to himself. His stomach grumbled with glee at the sight of the food.

"Thank you, Miss Gautier. You didn't have to do this. But what's in a po' boy sandwich?"

"Now, now, chile, no need to thank me. I said I was gon have you some good things to eat and I'm gonna keep my word. 'Cause I expect you to keep ya word, too," she said to him, her eyes smiling as they gazed over the top of her glasses. "Ain't that right?"

"Yes ma'am," Junebug caught himself smiling in response.

"And to answer ya question, a po' boy is a sandwich we make on French bread. Back home, a lot of the food come from the French people, on 'count of the French people that built that city way back when. We usually eat it with oysters, but I put you some shrimp on there. Try it and let me know how you like it. Well, you go ahead and I'm gonna go and get us some tools to work with out 'cheer. Just holla if you need anythin'."

Miss Gautier walked into the house and Junebug dove into the sandwich. The po' boy was good. He gobbled it down so quickly he surprised himself. The French bread was crusty so Junebug ended up with crumbs all over his shirt. Miss Gautier returned to the front porch just as he was swallowing the last bite. "How was everythin', baby?" She was struggling to carry a heavy basket in her right hand.

"It was good, thank you. The po' boy is my new favorite sandwich," said Junebug, wiping the last of the crumbs from his mouth and shirt. "Can I help you with that?"

"Oh, yes you can, 'fore I tip right over." Junebug took the basket from her. "So good to have a strong, young body 'round to help." She squeezed the muscle in his arm. "Mmm-hmm," she said to herself, still gripping Junebug's arm. Junebug looked up at her. She had the strangest look in her eyes. She jumped when she realized Junebug was watching her.

"Are you alright?" Junebug asked.

"Yeah, um - Yeah. Look here, I got a lil' project for us to work on. I wants to get my vegetable garden growin' again. I like to grow my own things to make one of my favorite dishes. You eat gumbo, boy?"

"What is that?" Junebug asked, frowning up his nose. He'd never heard of that but it didn't sound too good.

Miss Gautier laughed at his expression. "Well, it's some good eatin'. We make it where I'm from down in Lou's'ana. I talked about the French people in Nawleans but there were lots of people from Africa that built that city, too. And the food they brought with them was gumbo. It's got okra, which comes from Africa. It's got tomatoes and spice and different types of meat, shrimp and sausage. Real good, if you cook it right. How that sound to you?"

Junebug didn't know where 'Lou's'ana' was but the food Miss Gautier described sounded good to him. "I think I might like to try that."

"I thought you would, baby. I thought you would," Miss Gautier cooed, cracking a crooked smile. Her eyes had a peculiar twinkle. "Let's get going."

Miss Gautier's idea was to clear the underbrush in her yard and plant a new crop of her favorite vegetables. She wanted to plant a row of okra seeds, a row of tomato plants, something called sassafras, and some onions. Junebug spent the afternoon pulling weeds and dead grass to reveal the ground below. It was tough work. Even though Miss Gautier had given him gloves, and even though he tried to be careful, some of the thorns still made it through the gloves and stuck his fingers. At times it seemed that the more he pulled at the weeds, the

more of them appeared. Junebug was working up a
sweat. He stood up to wipe his forehead.

"You alright out there?" Miss Gautier asked from her
seat on her porch."Yes ma'am. Just hot," Junebug
shouted.

"When you get through with that patch over yonder,
I'll have a nice cool drink waiting on you."

Junebug gulped with anticipation. As he looked down, he noticed that, although he had just pulled weeds from the area he was standing in, there were vines around his ankles. Quickly he yanked his foot to try to get free but the vines didn't give. He tried again, jerking his leg, but the vines held fast and he lost his balance.

"Ouch!" Junebug scratched his elbow as he fell into a patch of thorns. Even with all that, the vines held on to his legs. Junebug began to kick his legs furiously. "Get offa me! Let me go!"

"What's the matter, baby?" Junebug looked up to see Miss Gautier standing on the sidewalk with a glass of lemonade in her free hand.

"I got tangled up in these vines. I thought I pulled them all up but I tripped over them."

"Yeah, baby, you gotta watch out for those vines," Miss Gautier said faintly. Junebug looked into her face. She stared at the ground and her mouth was moving. It was the first time he'd seen her with a frown on her face. What's more, Junebug noticed that her eyes had turned from their usual gray to green. She was whispering to herself but Junebug couldn't make out her words.

"Did you say something, Miss Gautier?"

Junebug's question broke Miss Gautier's concentration and she covered her mouth. "What you say, baby?"

"I thought you were saying something to me."

"Oh, no, no. But you try to get up now."

Junebug put his hands behind him and began to push himself up. As he glanced down at his feet he saw something very strange. It looked like the vines were falling away from his ankles. He blinked his eyes because he didn't believe what he was seeing. When Junebug looked down again, his legs were totally free.

"Did you see that?!!" Junebug spun around to Miss Gautier.

"See what, baby?" Her green eyes darted from the ground to him and back down.

"The vines. It was like they just melted away."

Miss Gautier chuckled. "Po' chile. You have been out here too long. Come here and get this lemonade quick," she laughed.

Still confused, Junebug began to move toward her while looking suspiciously at the ground and the plants where he'd been standing. As he got closer to Miss Gautier, Junebug looked up to take the glass of lemonade from her hand. He glanced into her face and noticed that her eyes were gray once again. Junebug wondered how Miss Gautier's eyes changed colors.

"Your eyes. They changed colors. What makes them do that?"

"Oh, I don't know, darlin'. Been that way most of my life. Change 'cording to how I'm feeling."

"Can you feel'em when they change?"

"Naw, can't say that I do. I guess it's just one of those things you can't control," Miss Gautier said as she looked at him, smiling with her eyes. "I want to thank you again for all of ya help. Look here, since you worked so hard, I cut you a hunk of the pound cake I made this morning. Here you go, baby. Now you save that 'til after dinner, 'cause I don't want ya mama fussing at me for ruining ya appetite."

Magically, all of Junebug's concern about the vines and the aches in his hands and back went away. Miss Gautier held the cake out to him and he took it and brought it to his nose. He could smell the sweet goodness through the paper towel. It reminded him of his Grandma Pearl. The way his mouth was watering, Junebug didn't think he could wait until after dinner.

"Alright, young mister, can I count on you to come back again tomorrow?" Miss Gautier asked. "I think I'll have some more Nawleans food for you to try. Maybe some little pecan candies we call pralines. Would you like that?"

"Yes ma'am. I like candy, and I like pecans, so I think I'll like pralines."

"Of course you will," she said. "Of course you will. You run on home now. See you tomorrow."

"Bye, Miss Gautier. See you tomorrow." Junebug picked up his backpack from the porch. He skipped down the sidewalk, out of the gate, and turned towards home. As he approached his house, Junebug stopped behind the big bush next to the driveway. He opened the paper towel and took a big bite out of the pound cake. Mmm! It was as good as it smelled. He chewed quickly and wiped his mouth as he walked in the front door.

"Mom, I'm home." From the smells and sounds, Junebug knew his mom was in the kitchen.

"Hey, Junebug! How was school today?" Gina asked as she bent down to kiss him on his forehead.

"It was cool."

"I saw you over there busting a sweat at Miss Gautier's. How did that go?"

"It went fine, but it was hard. I know I never want to be a farmer."

Gina smiled and giggled. "Oh really now?"

"Yeah. But Miss Gautier gave me good food. She made me a po' boy sandwich today. I'm going back tomorrow. She said she's making pralines."

"Looks like she found the right way to motivate you. You and that greedy gut of yours, boy."

CHAPTER 5

And so it went for the next several weeks. Junebug worked in Miss Gautier's gumbo garden nearly every day after he came home from school. Slowly, the tangled green mess that had been her front yard transformed into a lovely garden full of thriving plants and flowers. Pretty soon it became the talk of the neighborhood.

Before long, word got back to the neighborhood kids about what Junebug had been up to. Kareem was cool about it but Junebug had to hear it every day from Larry and Jenny. They started to call him "Zombie Boy." At lunch no one would swap food with him; they were all afraid that they would eat something that Miss Gautier the Hoo-Doo Witch made.

That's where they were wrong. If Junebug had anything in his lunchbox that Miss Gautier made, he would never offer to trade it. The one thing that made everything worth it – the hard work and the teasing – was Miss Gautier's good cooking. Nearly every day she had something new to offer Junebug for his trouble. One day it was homemade doughnuts she called beignets. Another day it was egg custard. And everything always tasted oh-so-good.

All that good eating made other areas of Junebug's life not-so-good. Because he was eating so much he was beginning to gain weight. None of his shirts covered his stomach and his pants wouldn't fasten. He had to take a deep breath before he bent over to tie his shoes. Things got so bad that his parents had to take him shopping for new clothes. Junebug couldn't even play kickball like he used to. The ball didn't go as far when he kicked it and it took him longer to get around the bases. Even though that was bad, it really didn't matter so much because Junebug was playing less and less at the park these days. Instead he was spending more and more time at Miss Gautier's, working in her gumbo garden.

On the other hand, Junebug had a good time at Miss Gautier's, and it wasn't just because of the good food. He liked being around her because she reminded him of Grandma Pearl. She always called him "sugar," or "sweetheart," and she always had a joke or funny story to share with him. Most of the time, Miss Gautier told Junebug about her life in Louisiana. According to her, she had been some type of nurse for the people in St. John's Parish, the area where she lived, like her mother and her mother's mother. People would come to her when they were feeling bad and she would use her knowledge of herbs to make them feel better. All of the things she knew made her a good gardener, too.

One day while they were sitting on Miss Gautier's porch polishing off some lemonade, Junebug asked her a question. "Why haven't we ever worked around that rosebush, Miss Gautier?"

"HHRRR-UMMMM," coughed Miss Gautier, choking on her last gulp of lemonade, her gray eyes darting from side to side. "What you say, baby?"

"Why haven't we worked on the rosebush over there?" he asked, pointing to the corner of the yard. "We've weeded around every other plant but that one."

"W-w-w-well," she stammered, "that is a very special plant. It was given to me by my mama and her mama to her before that. It is very delicate and I don't like anyone to work on it but me, so I don't want you ever to go over there, you hear?" Miss Gautier focused her gaze on Junebug. As he looked at her, he saw her eyes change from gray to green.

"Yes ma'am," he looked down into his glass. "But how come the roses on that bush are so big and red?"

"They are what they call blood roses, on account of the color. I use a special food on that plant to get the blooms that way."

"What kind of food?" Junebug asked, remembering something Larry had said about Miss Gautier's roses.

"Now, baby, that's a secret that was also handed down to me from my mama and by her mama to her." Her usual smile had dropped from her face. "You want some more lemonade?"

"N-n-no ma'am," Junebug stuttered, placing his glass on the table and making his way off of the porch. Miss Gautier's new mood made him uneasy.

"Wait a minute, sweetie. Come back here." Junebug spun around and saw Miss Gautier open the screen door and step inside the house. She turned around and handed Junebug a small brown sack. "Take this to ya mama. Tell her to take it as tea twice a day, with honey, and it'll help that upset stomach of hers. And these," she handed him something wrapped in cellophane, "are for you after ya dinner. Made a fresh batch of teacakes this afternoon."

"Thank you," he said shyly.

"Alright, now, I'll see you tomorrow, baby." With that, Junebug looked up and saw that Miss Gautier's smile had returned.

CHAPTER 6

The following afternoon Junebug returned to Miss Gautier's house. He had finished most of the work with the gumbo garden. Miss Gautier said it was up to nature to do the rest. Instead of working on the garden that day, Miss Gautier wanted Junebug to fertilize her flowers. Junebug was relieved; it was much easier to sprinkle than it was to dig and pull. She directed him to carefully sprinkle the white powder around the roots of the plants. He was to fertilize all the flowers along the fence and sidewalk but Miss Gautier warned Junebug to stay away from the rosebush. When he finished, she promised him some fresh beignets, which had become Junebug's favorite.

As he was working, Junebug noticed that Miss Gautier's front yard was in much better condition than it had been when he started working. He could actually walk through it without tripping on those pesky vines. Vegetables were beginning to appear on the plants he and Miss Gautier had cultivated. *It wouldn't be long,* Junebug thought to himself, *before the vegetables were ready for Miss Gautier's special gumbo.* He couldn't wait to taste it.

As Junebug walked along, whistling to himself and sprinkling the funny white powder, he noticed something strange lying on the ground next to the rosebush. *That's funny*, he thought. *I didn't see anything lying there when I came over this morning.* Junebug glanced towards the house to make sure Miss Gautier wasn't around. She wasn't on the porch so she must have been in the kitchen working on the beignets.

The coast was clear. Junebug began sprinkling and tiptoeing closer to the rosebush. The closer he came, he could see that there was some sort of strange doll laying on the ground under the rosebush. It was the size of his hand and made of black cloth. Someone had sewn on a face using white string. The doll had two small white "X"'s for eyes, like on the cartoons when the characters died. It had on a green top and brown shorts, the same color as his favorite outfit. He picked it up and noticed that it had stick pins pushed into it, some in its head, its neck, its arms, and chest. *That's weird*, Junebug thought. As he held the doll, he noticed a tag hanging down from a string attached to its leg. He grabbed the tag between his fingers and turned it over. Scrawled on it, in small letters, was one word – GREG.

Just then, Junebug heard noises coming from the bush. It sounded like chanting.

"Geechee Geechee ya ya, Geechee Geechee ya ya…"

"Who's there?" Junebug shouted.

"Geechee Geechee ya ya…"

"I said who's there?!" Junebug yelled. He realized the sound was coming from the hedges along the fence. "I hear you over there. Who are you?"

Just then Junebug heard giggling. Larry and Jenny jumped from behind the bush and onto the sidewalk. *"Geechee Geechee ya ya!"* they chanted in unison and then broke out laughing so hard they had to hold each other up.

"Did you see him, Jenny?" said Larry as water began to form in his eyes. "He was about to pee in his pants!"

"How do you like your hoo-doo doll?" Jenny sniggled. "We made that one but I know you-know-who has one of you, too. That's why you're over here all the time. She has you under her spell."

"NO SHE DOESN'T!" yelled Junebug. "Now get out of here!"

"Hey man, we were just having some fun," said Larry. "Don't get bent out of shape."

"I said, go!"

"Alright, Alright. Come on, Jenny, let's break out." They turned to walk away. "GEECHEE GEECHEE YA YA!" the two yelled in unison, and ran away laughing wildly.

"So stupid," Junebug said aloud as he stood there in Miss Gautier's yard holding the doll, watching Larry and Jenny run down the sidewalk. They just weren't going to let this thing with Miss Gautier go. Still, for a minute there, they had almost given him something to fear.

"Help us!"

Junebug spun around. He heard a strange, low voice calling out. *Not again*, he thought, making his way towards the hedges. "I thought I told you to leave me…" Junebug yelled into the hedges but as he peeked through them he realized there wasn't anyone on the other side. Confused, Junebug took a few steps back. *Is my mind playing tricks on me?*, he thought to himself.

"Help us!"

He heard it again. It was just above a whisper.

"Help us!"

This time it clearly sounded like more than one voice crying out in unison. His eyes darted from side to side, and he spun around in a circle, looking to see if anyone was standing nearby. Seeing no one, he looked down at the doll in his hand. Junebug lifted it to his ear to listen for a few seconds. Nothing. He threw the doll to the ground and shook his head in disbelief. Were Larry and Jenny getting inside of his head?

"*Help us!*"

This time there was no doubt. Someone or something was calling out to him. He looked around. There was no one he could see. Junebug turned towards the house and realized that he was standing next to the rosebush. He had never been so close to it before, except when he picked up the doll, and that had only been for a second. This was his first time really looking at the bush. Junebug wasn't one for flowers but the bush and the roses on it were beautiful. Even though it was the middle of the afternoon the leaves were dewy and bright green. The blooms were perfectly shaped and were the deepest color red that his eyes had ever seen. Grandma Pearl grew roses but they could not compare to these. He caught a hint of the roses' scent as a light wind blew. It was the old familiar smell of roses that reminded him of Grandma Pearl because she wore rose water as perfume.

Before he knew it he was drawn closer to the bush. With all the craziness he had just gone through, the scent of the roses was a pleasant change. Junebug took a step towards the bush and leaned in to take a whiff. As he did, he reached out and grabbed a bloom between his fingers.

"*Help us!*"

"Owww-eeee!" Junebug cried out, drawing his hand back in pain. He couldn't believe what he'd just heard. *The voices were coming from the bush!!! A talking rosebush?*

That was impossible!! Just then, Junebug realized that he was holding his hand, the one that had touched the bloom. He looked down and saw a trickle of blood running down from the tip of his finger. *Stupid thorns,* he thought to himself. Out of habit, he put his finger in his mouth to clean the blood. *I must be hearing things.* Junebug leaned over to the rosebush again, careful not to touch it this time. He turned his ear towards the bush.

"*Help us!*"

There was no doubt in his mind this time. Junebug took a step back and stared at the bush in disbelief. *Plants can't talk,* he thought. *Where was the voice coming from?* Very slowly, Junebug took a step forward as he continued to stare at the bush. Junebug focused in on one of the blooms. As he got closer, he couldn't believe his eyes. The bloom had eyes, a mouth...an entire face! It was staring back at him. He looked at another and it was the same thing. He walked all the way around the bush and each and every blossom spoke to him.

"*Help us!*" He saw the mouth of a rose move.

This couldn't be, this couldn't be. Junebug's mind began to race. *Bushes can't talk and roses can't talk and witches aren't real and neither is hoo-doo but I know I just saw what I saw and heard what I heard....*

Suddenly, Junebug's world went completely black.

* * * * * * *

"Junebug? Junebug, open your eyes!"

Junebug opened his eyes slowly. His vision was fuzzy but he could see his mother and father were standing over him.

"Oh, Junebug, are you alright?!" Gina asked.

"Y-y-yeah, I think so," he said, trying to sit up. When he did, he saw Miss Gautier standing behind his parents.

"You O.K., sweetheart?" Miss Gautier asked.

"Yes ma'am."

"I know you were workin' hard, but I didn't think you was working *that* hard," Miss Gautier chuckled. "You plum fainted out here, boy. You better go home and lie down. Get you some rest."

"That sounds like some good advice," Greg, Sr. smiled.

"As a matter of fact, I got somethin' in the house that might help 'em. Give me one minute." Miss Gautier spun around and hobbled back toward the house using her cane.

"Come on, Junie, let's get you off the ground." Gina threw Junebug's arm over her shoulder and lifted him from his waist.

Junebug's head was still spinning. *What happened?* All he remembered was sprinkling the fertilizer.

"Frankly, I'm proud of you, son. I didn't know you had it in you to work that hard," laughed Greg, Sr., as he threw fake punches at Junebug's stomach.

Junebug blocked the punches and smiled. "Me either."

"Are you sure that you feel alright?," Gina asked as she brushed the dirt from the back of Junebug's head and shoulders.

"Gina, he's fine. Hard work is good for a growing boy."

"Here it is," said Miss Gautier, making her way back from the house. She had two paper bags in her hand, one speckled with what looked like grease stains. "Now Gina," she said, handing one bag to his mother, "make him a lil' tea with this. It's some chamomile and mint, help settle the stomach. Then later," she handed her the other bag, "after he feels better, you can give him these. Those the beignets I promised him for his work today. I'm just so sorry he fell out. I feel so bad."

"Oh, that's alright, Miss Gautier," said Greg, Sr. "We'll make sure he takes the tea and gets some rest."

"Oh, alright now," Miss Gautier said. "Now, don't worry about comin' over tomorrow. We'll just get back to things when you got ya strength back." She reached over and rubbed the top of Junebug's head.

Junebug gave her a slight smile. Some memories were coming back to him. He remembered Larry and Jenny and the stupid doll.

"Come on, son, let's go home," said Greg, Sr.

As Junebug made his way home, he tried to remember what had happened to him. His mom and dad took him to his room and made him lay down. Gina brought him some of the tea Miss Gautier sent over. After he finished it, Junebug laid in the bed, drifting off to sleep. He didn't feel that sleepy on the way home but after he drank the tea, Junebug could feel his entire body relax. Slowly, he could feel his insides begin to heat up. The feeling moved up his body through his neck to his head. Junebug could feel sweat breaking out on his forehead. Even though he was lying on the bed, his bedroom felt like it was spinning in circles. Junebug closed his eyes to try and stop the motion. When he did, he began to see images. He saw the rosebush. Then another image came to his mind. He saw Toussaint, Miss Gautier's cat, sitting on his chest, staring into his face. The cat's eyes were a bright, glowing green. *That's strange*, Junebug thought. *Toussaint hardly ever comes near me.* As he drifted closer and closer to sleep, he wasn't sure if he was remembering or imagining these things.

"Roses are red and grass is green, disremember the things that you just seen."

Junebug opened his eyes. "Who said that?" he mumbled to himself. There wasn't anyone else in the room, but he could have sworn…

"Rose are red and grass is green, you don't remember the things that you just seen."

Who? What? Junebug opened his eyes again, searching the room. Things were spinning around so fast that he was beginning to feel queasy, so he closed his eyes again. *Too weird,* he thought to himself. *Too weird.* Slowly, Junebug drifted off to sleep.

CHAPTER 7

When Junebug woke up the next morning he felt as right as rain, as his Grandma Pearl would say. He barely remembered anything about the day before. Things started off well because his mom let him have yesterday's beignets for breakfast since he slept all night.

On the way to school that morning, things took a turn for the worse. Of course Larry and Jenny had blabbed their big mouths to Kareem about the prank they played on him. Even though Kareem didn't believe the things the two of them said about Miss Gautier, he giggled when they told him about the hoo-doo doll.

"That was cold," he giggled. "You alright, man?" he asked Junebug.

"I'm cool," he answered. "You just need to tell your friends to chill."

"We were just having some fun," said Jenny. "Can't you take a joke?"

"I've had enough your jokes," Junebug said.

"Look, Greg, we are just trying to open your eyes to the truth. We're trying to save you, but I think it's too late. Besides, if Miss Gautier doesn't steal your soul, it looks like she's going to feed you until you bust." With that, Larry poked his finger into Junebug's swollen belly and chuckled like the Pillsbury Doughboy. All three of them began to laugh hysterically, except Junebug.

"That's alright! Go ahead and laugh! Ya'll just jealous!" Junebug yelled. Despite his yelling, Larry, Jenny, and Kareem couldn't hear him over their own laughter.

After that, the crew stopped teasing Junebug as much and things went back to normal. In a few days he started back working at Miss Gautier's and, as usual, she began making her special treats for him. Jelly cookies. Brownies. Something called red velvet cake.

Before long, school let out for the summer. The vegetables in Miss Gautier's gumbo garden began to ripen. That meant Miss Gautier would be making her special gumbo real soon.

As the days went by, Junebug grew more and more excited by the prospect of harvest time. Miss Gautier even said she would let him help her cook. That meant that Junebug would get to taste the ingredients along every step of the way. He was starting to think that he wanted to be a chef when he grew up.

Finally the big day came. Junebug let his parents know that he would be next door for most of the day.

"O.K., baby," said Gina. "Just make sure you are on your best behavior." She kissed Junebug on the forehead before he ran out of the door.

Junebug sprinted next door and burst through the gate, running down the sidewalk as fast as his chubby legs would carry him. He banged on the door to let Miss Gautier know that he was there.

"Hey, chile," she crowed through the screen door. "Today is the day. You ready?"

"Um-hmm!" Junebug could barely hide his excitement.

"Just give me a minute, sugar, and let me get my things." After a few minutes she returned to the door and stepped out on the porch. She had on her straw hat again and her eyes were a sparkling greenish-gray. She had her cane in one hand and a big straw basket hanging over her opposite arm. As she stood on the porch, Toussaint wove himself between her ankles.

Junebug and Miss Gautier headed out to the garden. As they got started, she showed him how to gently remove the okra and tomatoes from the plants so they wouldn't get bruised. She also showed him how to dig up the onions and garlic.

Considering all the work it had taken to clear the ground and wait for the plants to grow, it didn't take any time for the two of them to pluck the plants clean. Within a few minutes, Miss Gautier's basket was overflowing with vegetables.

"I think that'll do it, my friend," she said to Junebug as she struggled to carry the basket. "Now let's get cookin'."

Junebug followed her out of the garden patch. He almost tripped over Toussaint, who had suddenly become very friendly towards him. While they were working in the garden, Toussaint constantly rubbed himself against Junebug's legs. He never could figure that cat out.

As they step onto the porch, Junebug realized this would be his first time going inside Miss Gautier's house.

"Come on in, baby," she said as they reached the screen door. Her eyes had turned completely green by then.

Junebug stepped inside the front room. *Yep*, he said to himself, *it smells like an old lady's house* – like mothballs and ointment and flowery perfume. There was a sofa and big chairs along the wall, all covered in plastic. In front of the sofa was a coffee table covered with crocheted dollies and knick-knacks. Underneath the table lay an oval-shaped braided rug. There were shelves and tables all around the room, covered with figurines in the shapes of angels and animals. Junebug noticed, however, that there weren't any pictures anywhere. *Dad said she probably didn't have any family,* he thought to himself. *Or maybe her pictures got damaged in the hurricane.*

Miss Gautier stopped next to the door and placed her basket on the floor. She untied her hat and when she did her braids fell to her shoulders. For some reason, maybe because of the dimly lit room, her hair didn't seem as gray as Junebug remembered. She hung her hat on the rack next to the door and leaned her cane against the doorjamb.

"I won't need that old thing in here. Come on, baby, let's go to the kitchen. Straight down the hall, here. Just follow Toussaint."

Junebug turned around and saw that the cat was already halfway down the hall. The walls of the hall were covered with white wallpaper with small yellow flowers. As he moved down the hall, everything became duller and dingier. There was so little light that he could barely see Toussaint's dark body at all. The cat stopped and turned around, fixing his green eyes on Junebug.

"Meeeoooww!," he said. Junebug could have sworn the crazy cat smiled at him. As he came closer, Toussaint sat up and galloped further down the hall, and then disappeared into a door on the right.

Junebug turned around and saw Miss Gautier limping down the hall behind them, carrying the vegetable basket in her hand and balancing herself against the wall.

"Go on," she said. "Toussaint's showing you the way."

When he reached the end of hall, Junebug saw where the cat went. There was a flight of narrow steps leading down to the basement. It took a few seconds for his eyes to adjust to the dim light, but after he did, Junebug held the handrail and carefully stepped down, down, down the stairs.

"Your kitchen is in the basement?," he called back to Miss Gautier.

"Yeah, baby. This an old house."

This part of the house smelled different. There was a hint of some of the familiar spices Miss Gautier used in her cooking and baking, like cinnamon, pepper, and vanilla. But there were other smells that he couldn't make out. The air seemed heavy and wet, like there was something boiling.

As Junebug continued down the steps he noticed that Miss Gautier's kitchen looked more like a laboratory. There wasn't enough light in the room to see very well. There were small windows along the top of the walls, but they had been overgrown by weeds, so the light that came in was dim and green. There were shelves all along the wall, which were covered with jars and containers in various shapes, sizes, and colors. All around dried plants hung from strings. Over in the corner of the room was a funny-shaped old stove with a fire burning inside. Next to it was a pile of firewood stacked halfway the wall. There was a big wooden table in the middle of the room, over which hung a rack with pots and pans of all sizes.

Junebug heard Miss Gautier creaking down the stairs behind him.

"Baby, help me put this basket on the table."

He took it from her hand and the basket immediately hit the ground. Junebug dragged it across the floor to the table and then, using all his strength, managed to get it on top of the table. He pulled a chair out from the table and sat down to catch his breath.

"What are we going to do first?" Junebug couldn't hide the excitement in his voice.

"Well, sweetness," Miss Gautier giggled, "let me get my pot down first and we'll see. Can you cut the veggies?"

"Ummm, yeah. Momma lets me cut stuff in the kitchen all the time," Junebug lied.

"O.K. then." Miss Gautier moved some things around on the big table and pulled out a big, flat piece of wood and sat it down in front of Junebug. She turned back around and placed a knife on top of the board. "Let me rinse the okra off and you can start with that." Junebug watched her as she grabbed two handfuls of the long, green pods and ran water over them under the faucet in the deep, white sink. Miss Gautier shook them until they stopped dripping and sat them on the board in front of him.

"Now make sure you cut off the ends. Then you wanna cut'em in pieces 'bout an inch long. Can you handle that?"

That sounds easy enough, Junebug thought to himself. "Sure," he said confidently, taking the knife into his right hand.

"Now be careful. That knife is sharp." Miss Gautier reached up over the table and pulled a string. Junebug jumped at the sound of the clattering pans as they lowered from the ceiling. Miss Gautier took the biggest, blackest pot on the rack down, filled it with water, and placed it on the stove. It was a huge pot, big enough for Junebug to sit down in. He could hardly believe that the old lady could lift it by herself. It landed on the stove with a loud clank. She took out another board and knife and began to cut some of the other ingredients while she stood at the table.

Miss Gautier took some garlic and onions and cut them up, humming to herself all the while. She was working so furiously that the two braids she wore her hair in began to come undone. Junebug noticed again that somehow her hair didn't seem as gray in the basement light.

Just then Toussaint jumped from the floor to the table and startled Junebug just as he was coming down with the knife on a pod of okra.

"Owww!" he cried clutching his finger. He looked and saw that he had cut the skin on the tip of his finger.

"Oh, oh," Miss Gautier said. "What's the matter?"

"I cut my finger," Junebug said, holding his hand out for her to inspect.

"You hold it just a minute." Miss Gautier shuffled to the far corner of the basement. She reached into the corner and grabbed something Junebug couldn't see. As she came back, he noticed that she wasn't limping at all.

"Let me see your hand." She took his finger and put a spongy, gray clump on the cut.

"What's that?" Junebug asked.

"It's some spider's web."

"S-s-spider's web?!!" Junebug jumped up and tried to snatch his hand back, but Miss Gautier's grip was too strong.

"Calm down, boy. Ain't no spider, just the web. It'll stop the bleeding."

"You don't have any band-aids?"

"This better than a band-aid. See?" She lifted up the clump of web and showed it his finger. The blood was gone. All he could see was a small pink slit where his skin was split. "Now you see?"

Junebug could see alright. As he looked at Miss Gautier, he noticed that she almost looked like a completely different person. Her face was usually covered with wrinkles, but now her skin was almost completely smooth and creamy. Even her hands, that now held Junebug's, were not as rough as they usually were. She hardly looked like an old woman anymore.

Miss Gautier noticed Junebug's staring eyes. "You'll be alright," she said as she moved back to her spot at the table. She reached over and gave Junebug a bowl. "Put them okra pieces in here and you get started on them tomatoes."

She headed over to attend to the boiling pot on the wood stove. Miss Gautier moved around the room, pinching leaves from the hanging bundles, and scooping from various jars and adding it all to the big, black pot. The smell of the spices became heavy in the room and the steam only added to the dimness. As he continued to chop tomatoes it seemed as if the room was filled with fog. Even though Miss Gautier was standing near him at the counter, he could barely see her, instead he listened for her footsteps around the room.

"Miss Gautier, I'm finished with the tomatoes," Junebug said. There was no reply. He looked around, but couldn't see across the room through all of the steam. "Miss Gautier?" Still no answer.

"Rrrreeeernnnn!" Junebug jumped at the sound of Toussaint's low growl. It came from some far corner of the kitchen.

"Miss G, where are you?" Junebug stood up from the table and tried to feel his way towards the steps. Maybe she had to go upstairs for something. He followed the edge of the table as far as he could and stuck his left hand into the cloudy whiteness to feel around for anything he might run into.

"Ahhhhhh!" Junebug jumped as he felt something soft rubbing against his leg. He looked down and saw black fur passing next to his leg. Toussaint again. "Stupid cat!" Junebug said under his breath. He could feel his heart thumping in his chest.

"He's not so stupid, chile."

Junebug jumped and his head shot up. There was a young woman with green eyes and creamy skin standing directly in front of him. Her long, black hair fell in curls over her shoulders and onto her dress, a dress that looked just like the one Miss Gautier was wearing.

"Who - who are you? Where's Miss Gautier?" Junebug stuttered.

"Right here in front of you, boy." She put her hand on his shoulder and squeezed him so hard he cringed. She bent over, placing her face in front of his. Her eyes! Her eyes were the same as Miss Gautier but they were dancing green.

"We got some gumbo to finish," she said, smiling widely. Junebug shivered under her touch.

CHAPTER 8

"W-w-w-what are you doing?" Junebug screamed.

"Calm down, baby. We just gon finish what we started." She grabbed him by both of his shoulders and lifted him, effortlessly, into the air. She inhaled deeply and blew her breath over him. It was like a strong wind and it cleared the room of all steam. Junebug's eyes widened with amazement. The room had been totally transformed. It was still very dark but he could see things that weren't there before. There were burning candles all around the room on the wall. There were pictures of people dressed up like in olden times, with strings of shells and feathers hanging beneath them. The whole place smelled like mud and leaves. There were shelves with all kinds of skeletons that looked like they belonged to alligators and small lizards. He dropped his gaze and right next to the shelf he saw a pile of snakes slithering about on the floor. In fact, snakes were everywhere he looked, on the shelves, curling around the legs of tables and chairs.

"What are you going to do to me?" Junebug felt his heart move into his throat.

"Haven't you heard anything I've said? We've got to finish what we started. It's time to finish the gumbo." Miss Gautier, or the woman who said she was Miss Gautier, smiled broadly from ear to ear. She looked so young that she could have been his mother's age.

Junebug gulped. "I already did my part. I-I-I cut the okra and-and-and the tomatoes."

Miss Gautier cackled. "But, sweetness, you forgot the best part." The smile dropped from her face and she stared through Junebug with her cold green eyes. "My gumbo won't be complete without the meat from a sweet little boy."

"Huh?!! No, no, no!" Junebug couldn't wrap his mind around what was happening. Larry and Jenny *had* been right. Miss Gautier was a witch and now she was going to eat him!

Junebug tried to get out of her grip but she held him tight. She began to move across the dank room into one of the far corners. She opened the door on a small cage on the floor. She pushed Junebug into it and slammed the door shut.

"Now, you stay put." She walked back towards the stove. Junebug placed his hand on the door of the cage and began to push it open. "I wouldn't do that if I were you," she said in a low voice without turning around. "Remember, you've got company." Just then, Junebug looked down and saw that the snakes had left their pile and surrounded the outside of the cage. When he tried to place his foot outside of the cage, they stood upright and tried to bite him.

"Aaaiiieee!" Junebug cried. He wasn't afraid of many things, but he hated snakes. "Let me go! Let me out of here!" Junebug yelled, his voice quivering with fear as he fought to hold back tears.

"Don't worry, sugar. I'll be ready for you in a minute." Miss Gautier continued to move about the kitchen tossing things here and there into the big, black pot. She hummed gleefully to herself. Just then there was a knock at the door.

"I wonder who this could be." She placed the lid on the big pot. "Keep an eye on him while I go take care of this, Toussaint" she said, looking towards a dark corner of the room.

"Yes, madam." Junebug couldn't see who was talking but as he stared at the darkness in the corner, a set of bright green eyes appeared and moved towards him. Instead of the cat, a short man emerged out of the dark. He couldn't have been any taller that Junebug and he wore a loincloth like Junebug had seen the Indians in his school books. He had a necklace made of what looked like animal teeth around his neck.

Although his body was different, Junebug would recognize those eyes anywhere. How did a cat turn into a man? Junebug was as confused as he was scared. Just then he noticed Miss Gautier going up the stairs. Although the light was not the best, he could see that as she went farther and farther up the stairs, her hair became lighter and lighter, and it twirled itself into the braids he was used to seeing her with. She opened the door to leave the lair.

"Don't leave me down here! Let me go!" Junebug yelled.

"I'm coming. I'm coming," crowed Miss Gautier in her old woman voice. He could hear her shuffling footsteps as she walked down the hall towards the door.

"Hey, Miss Gautier. How are you?"

Junebug recognized the voice quickly. It was his mother. He could hear Jack-Jack barking.

"I was just wondering if you'd seen lil' Greg."

"I'M HERE, MAMA! I'M HERE!" Junebug screamed at the top of his lungs. Just then Toussaint ran over to the cage, grabbed Junebug by the arm, and covered his mouth with his little, grimy hands.

"MMMMM! MMMM!" he tried to shout through Toussaint's grip but it was no use.

"Well, no, I haven't seen him for a while now. Think he said he was going down to the park to play with some of the other children. You know how little boys are. He ought to be back later this afternoon. You should go home and wait for him."

"MMMMM! MMMMM!" Junebug tried again to yell. If he couldn't get his mom to hear him, it might just be the end of him. "MMMMM!"

"Pipe down, now, you," Toussaint hissed as he struggled to muffle Junebug. Suddenly Junebug had an idea. "Owww!" Toussaint screamed as Junebug bit his fingers.

"MOM! MOM! I'M DOWN HERE!"

"Alright, Miss Gautier, but if you see him before I do, send him right home please." Junebug could hear Jack-Jack barking fiercely. "I don't know what's gotten into this dog," said Gina.

"JACK-JACK! HELP ME, HELP ME!" Junebug yelled again. Jack-Jack barked even louder but suddenly Junebug heard the front door slam shut.

It seemed that the door had closed on Junebug's only chance at freedom.

CHAPTER 9

Junebug sat down in the corner of his holding pen and tried to fight back the tears. What would become of him now? It seemed like Miss Gautier was determined to put him in her gumbo. And why didn't he listen to Larry and Jenny? Now he would never see his parents again. Or his Grandma Pearl. Or his cousins. Or Jack-Jack.

Jack-Jack! He was the only one who knew where he was, but Junebug didn't know how he could get into Miss Gautier's house.

Just then, Junebug heard the sound of shuffling feet. It was Miss Gautier coming back to the basement.

"Now that we got the distractions out of the way, Toussaint, let's me and you and our friend here 'tend to our business."

Junebug gulped. "Leave me alone!"

"Hush ya fuss, chile. It'll be over 'fore you know it," she said with an evil grin across her face as she stood over the steaming pot. "Toussaint!"

"Yes, madam," Toussaint answered as he slowly stepped forward out of a dark corner of the room.

"I need you to go out on the back porch and get some sassafras I got drying out there. That'll be the last thing we need for our feast."

"Yes, madam," he said, turning for the steep, steep stairs. Junebug stared in amazement as he watched

Toussaint go up the stairs. With each step, his features changed. He grew fur, and his back slumped over and his arms became feet. By the time he reached the top of the stairs, he was the same black cat Junebug knew. Once he reached the top of the stairs, Toussaint turned right towards the back door that led to the backyard. Junebug heard the sound of the door opening as Toussaint went out back.

Junebug crouched in a corner of his little cell. Slowly, a feeling of hopelessness crept over him. He peered out between the bars to see Miss Gautier, the young version, whisking back and forth across the room, grabbing this bottle and shaking that jar, and stirring the pot in between with a big, wooden spoon that went *cling, cling* against its sides. He could hear the sound of her feet moving across the floor and her light, almost joyful humming as she went about her evil work. Underneath it all he could also hear the low slithering and sliding of what seemed like hundreds of insects, and dozens of snakes that covered the floor. *What a terrible way for my life to end,* he thought to himself.

Just as he began to envision his own funeral, Junebug heard noises coming from upstairs. There was very loud barking and hissing. He would have recognized that bark anywhere: it was Jack-Jack! *He did hear me,* thought Junebug. "Jack-Jack! I'm down here! I'm down here!"

"What the devil!," exclaimed Miss Gautier as she stopped the clanking of her pots and listened. "Toussaint, you alright out there?"

The sounds of the fight continued but gradually he heard less and less hissing. Suddenly all went silent.

"Toussaint?! Toussaint come on in here now!" demanded Miss Gautier as she began to make her way up the stairs.

Just then they heard the sound of the door swing on its hinges and the sound of something walking across the floor in the hall.

Miss Gautier stopped in the middle of the staircase. "'Bout time you get back in here!" she yelled. "We ain't got no time for you to be foolin' 'round with that dog! We got gumbo to make!" She turned on her heels and headed back down the stairs.

Junebug grabbed the bars and stared at the door. It was quiet. Suddenly, he saw a dark figure at the top of the stairs. Then he heard a low, mean growl.

"Jack-Jack!" Junebug shouted. "Attack!"

Before Miss Gautier could turn around Jack-Jack leaped from the top of the stairs onto her back.

"Get her, Jack-Jack, get her!"

Jack-Jack sunk his teeth into her neck as she began to fall down the stairs. The dog rode her like a surfboard all the way to the bottom of the stairs. They hit the basement floor with a loud thump. Jack-Jack jumped off Miss Gautier's back and stood over her growling, waiting for her to get up. But she didn't move. Not one muscle.

Jack-Jack sniffed around her until he was satisfied and came over to where Junebug's cage. He barked and snarled at the snakes that had been holding Junebug captive and made a path to the cell. Once the floor was clear, Junebug leaped from the cage and hugged Jack-Jack around the neck.

"Oh, thank you, thank you! You saved my life! That crazy lady was going to eat me!" Jack-Jack just licked Junebug all over his face. "Come on, let's get out of here!" Junebug led Jack-Jack to the stairs. He looked down at Miss Gautier's motionless body. "I guess that means no gumbo for you," Junebug laughed and stepped over Miss Gautier.

"Not so fast, chile." Before he knew what was happening, Miss Gautier grabbed Junebug by the leg.

"Oh no!" he screamed.

Jack-Jack bit her arm. "Aaaahhhh!" she cried in pain, as she released Junebug's ankle. He scrambled to his feet and ran to the opposite side of the kitchen behind some of the shelves. He watched as she managed to lift herself from the floor. Jack-Jack lunged at her, grabbing hold of her skirt. Miss Gautier searched the room with her wild eyes until she stopped them on Junebug.

"You!!!" she screamed and tried to take off in his direction, only to be stopped by Jack-Jack's grip on her dress. "Let me go!" she yelled at him, as she tried to snatch her dress from his jaws. She tugged and tugged and with the last pull there was a loud rip. Jack-Jack tumbled backward with the corner of her dress still between his teeth, crashing into a shelf in the corner. Several boxes fell onto Jack-Jack. Junebug could hear him yelping as he tried to get free but he was stuck.

Miss Gautier looked over in the corner at Jack-Jack, and then turned towards Junebug.

"Oh no!" Junebug gasped as she came towards him.

"Ya dog tried to help you but I ain't through with you yet, lil' boy," Miss Gautier hissed as she stepped closer and closer. There was nowhere to hide. Miss Gautier stood between Junebug and the basement door.

"No! Let me go home!" whined Junebug. He ran behind the stove looking for something to defend himself. Thinking quickly, he grabbed a piece of firewood.

"Go home?" she growled, stepping in front of the stove. "We've still got to finish our gumbo."

In a flash, Junebug pushed the end of the firewood against the stove and pushed with all his might. "I got your gumbo for you!" The stove leaned over and the boiling hot gumbo spilled out of the pot and splashed onto Miss Gautier, covering her from head to toe.

"NOOOOOOOO! NOOOOOO!"

Junebug kept pushing until the stove fell completely over, pinning Miss Gautier to the floor beneath its weight. Junebug stepped around the stove onto a box to escape the steaming liquid as it flowed over the floor. From his perched position, he had a better view of Miss Gautier struggling on the floor.

"NOOOOO! AHHHH!" she yelled and wriggled under the weight and heat of the stove and the gumbo. Just then, Junebug noticed that the gumbo wasn't the only thing steaming. Miss Gautier seemed to be evaporating into a green fog.

"NOOOOOO!" she screamed, but it did nothing to stop her from melting, melting, melting slowly away. Her body became streaks of greenish-brown ooze flowing along the floor, mixed with the pieces of chopped okra and onions. "NOOOOO! NOOOOO! GRRRRRRR-!" Junebug backed away from the hot, sizzling mess on the floor. He turned his eyes away for Miss Gautier's disappearing body. Finally there was nothing left but her dress floating in the stew. Miss Gautier was no more.

Junebug could barely take his eyes of the bubbling goop that had been Miss Gautier, but there was no time for celebration. "Gross!" Junebug said to himself, mostly out of relief. Out of the corner of his eye Junebug noticed flames behind him. Embers from the stove had spread to the wood pile and the entire stack of wood was burning. Within seconds, the flames grew higher and higher, spreading to the dried herbs and roots hanging around the room, to the boxes and crates. The room was quickly filling with smoke. Junebug knew he had to get out before the entire house went up in flames.

But what about Jack-Jack? Carefully, Junebug jumped from the box on which he had been standing and ran over to the corner. "Hang on, Jack-Jack, I'm coming!" With that Junebug began to dig in the pile of boxes until Jack-Jack had enough room to get out. The dog stepped out slowly and stood for a moment before he began to shake the dust from his fur. He looked around the room for a moment, growling lowly and then barking.

"It's O.K., Jack-Jack," said Junebug, beginning to cough. "Miss Gautier is gone, but the fire! Come on!" Junebug stood up, pulling Jack-Jack's collar, and started for the stairs. He could hear the roar of the fire as it spread around the room. Junebug covered his nose and mouth with the crook of his arm to stop breathing in the smoke, but he kept coughing. By the time he reached the top of the stairs, he could hardly see the steps in front of him, but he could feel Jack-Jack moving up the stairs beside him. Junebug reached out and grabbed hold of his tail and let Jack-Jack guide him to the door.

Finally, they reached the top of the stairs. Junebug stumbled over the last step and fell into the hallway. He coughed and coughed but was finally able to fill his lungs with fresh air as he lay on the floor. After a few deep breaths, Junebug looked up and saw that the hallway was beginning to fill with smoke. It wouldn't be long before the entire house caught on fire.

"Arrhfff! Arrhff!" Jack-Jack was standing over Junebug. He reached down and grabbed him by the collar and began to pull him toward the door. Junebug was able to make it to his hands and knees. Jack-Jack let him go and they both crawled along the floor under the billowing cloud of smoke, towards the front door. Junebug stood up, flung the door open, and he and Jack-Jack ran as fast as they could down the sidewalk.

Junebug's eyes were watering from the smoke but as he ran through the yard, he noticed something very strange. The plants in Miss Gautier's garden were glowing. He stopped running and stared at the rosebush in the corner of the yard. It was glowing bright red, and then suddenly it was consumed by green smoke. Slowly the smoke cleared and he could hardly believe his eyes! There where the bush had been were five children. They all appeared to be about his age. They seemed to be as confused as Junebug was, and they stood staring at their arms and touching themselves in disbelief. Next, they looked around at each other and then at the burning house. One by one, the boys and girls of the rosebush, one of which Junebug was certain had to be Dennis Muldrow, hopped over the fence and ran away.

Junebug looked to his right and saw green mist and then dozens upon dozens of cats, dogs, and birds standing where the mist had been. For a moment, they stood silently, staring at each other, but all at once they let loose a collective roar of meows, barks, and chirping. The birds took off into the air into what seemed to be a cloud of feathers, while the cats and dogs began a stampede toward the gate, trampling over each other in the process. The entire garden, it seems, had been made up of living victims that Miss Gautier had lured to her home. Junebug snapped out of his disbelief after nearly being pushed down by the crowd of animals running past his legs. He took off through the gate, and ran towards his house.

Once in the safety of his yard, Junebug looked at Miss Gautier's house. Jack-Jack stood beside him, barking at the house. Smoke was coming from all of the windows and the smell of burning wood was in the air. He had learned at school to call 911 if something like this happened but somehow he thought the best thing to do was to let this fire burn. He wanted to make sure Miss Gautier was gone forever. Before long, some of the other neighbors smelled the smoke and were standing on their porches and the sidewalk watching the blaze consume the house. After a few minutes, Junebug heard the sound of a fire engine approaching. It was about that same time that Gina came running from their house.

"Baby, are you alright?!" she grabbed Junebug by the shoulders, looking at him from head to toe. She hugged him tightly and then looked at him again. "Why are you so dirty? And you smell like smoke. You weren't trying to save Miss Gautier, were you?"

"Mom -"

By that time, Greg, Sr. had come from the house and was standing over Junebug and his mother. "Junebug!" he grabbed him by the shoulders. "You shouldn't have tried to be a hero. What if you were trapped in the house? I know you were attached to Miss Gautier, but you call for help. You don't try to do it yourself!"

"But-"

"I'm just so glad you're alright, but poor Miss Gautier!" Gina stopped squeezing Junebug long enough to look over the fence. The firemen were pulling the hose towards the house but the whole building looked like one big fireball. They sprayed and sprayed and were eventually able to put out the flames. In the end there was nothing left of the house, Toussaint, or Miss Gautier.

CHAPTER 10

For the next few weeks, the mysterious fire on Juniper Street was the topic of conversation among the town's people. The fire marshal determined that the cause of the fire was the wood burning stove in the basement of Miss Gautier's house. Most assumed that the fire must have started while she was baking some of her famous goodies. The mystery remained however because they never found Miss Gautier's body in the rubble, which was very strange.

Even more bizarre was the sudden appearance of several children who had been missing for a few months, and more than a few dozen pet cats and dogs. The local paper was filled with accounts of reunited families, happy to have their children at home. None of the children, however, could remember where they had been for all those weeks, and the parents were so happy that no one really cared, as long as they were home again.

After a few weeks, the drama of Miss Gautier's house began to die down and things on Juniper Street returned to normal. Junebug put all memories of Miss Gautier behind him, and after a while the other children grew tired of teasing him about her. He finally had to admit to Jenny and Larry that they had been right about Miss Gautier. After the whole event, Junebug began spending more and more time at the community park with Larry, Jenny, and Kareem, and regained his record as the kickball champion. Now that he wasn't eating sweet goodies every day, Junebug even lost a few pounds.

Things at home with the Joneses were good, too. Before long, someone bought the land where Miss Gautier's house had once stood. Within a few months, a new house stood next door, and new neighbors moved in not long after. Junebug hadn't seen them yet, but he overheard his mother and father discussing that they were an older couple.

One day, Junebug returned home from playing at the park to find that his parents had invited the new neighbors over for dinner. "Junebug," Gina said as he walked through the door, "go upstairs and wash up for dinner. We are having guests."

"Who?" he asked.

"You'll get to meet them soon enough. Go clean up, quick," Gina responded.

Junebug bounded up the stairs to wash his face and hands. Behind him he heard the doorbell ring, then new voices along with those of his parents. After he finished, he bounced back downstairs. There he ran into Jack-Jack who was whimpering and walking in circles at the foot of the stairs.

"What's wrong, boy?" Junebug kneeled to pet him. Jack-Jack startled Junebug by barking towards the kitchen. "What's in the kitchen, Jack-Jack? What are you trying to tell me? Huh, boy?" Junebug stroked Jack-Jack and tried to calm him.

"Greg Jr., in here," his dad called from the dining room. "I'd like you to meet Mr. and Mrs. Rillieux, our new neighbors. They just moved here from Texas."

"How do you do, son?" Mr. Rillieux said to Junebug, reaching out his hand. Junebug pushed the thoughts of Miss Gautier that rose in his mind away, and met Mr.

Rillieux's grip. His head was bald on top and he had silver hair around the sides and back of his head. He wore silver-rimmed glasses. Mr. Rillieux smiled as Junebug took his wrinkled brown hand and shook it. He seemed nice enough, Junebug thought.

"Good to meet you, Greg Jr.," Mrs. Rillieux patted Junebug on the head. She had silver hair, too, but she had pulled hers back into a bun that rested on the back of her head. She was the color of those caramel chews his mom bought from the store, but her eyes! Her eyes were an eerie shade of gray that reminded him of...

"Alright, folks, let's dig in!" said Greg, Sr. Everyone pulled out their chairs and sat down at the table. Junebug noticed a big ceramic pot sitting in the middle of the table. The scent was familiar but he couldn't remember where he'd smelled it before.

"What's in the pot?" Junebug asked.

"Well, we invited the Rillieuxes over for dinner but they insisted on cooking for us. Smells delicious doesn't it? What did you say it was again?"

"Well," Mrs. Rillieux said, her gray eyes beginning to gleam, "it's a recipe that's been in the family for years. My mother learned it from her mother. It's one of the favorite dishes from back home in New Orleans."

"New Orleans?" Junebug asked as his eyes stretched. "I thought you said you were from Texas."

"Oh, well, we lived in Texas for years, but we were born and raised in New Orleans," said Mr. Rillieux.

"But even in Texas, people loved our special gumbo," Mrs. Rillieux said proudly.

"GUMBO!" cried Junebug. "NOT GUMBO!" He shot up out of his chair. He could feel his heartbeat speeding up. It was so loud he could hear it in his ears.

"Junebug!" Gina exclaimed. "Where are your manners?! I know it's different but you ought to give new things a try."

"Ummm – Sorry. I don't mean to be rude." Junebug thought fast. "I-I-I'm just not that hungry right now. I had something to eat at Kareem's house. May I-I-I be excused, please?"

Gina looked at Greg. Greg shook his head and shrugged his shoulders. The Rillieuxs looked at each other and then at Greg and Gina. Jack-Jack stood at the entrance to the dining room whimpering.

"Well, alright Junie. You're excused. Since you aren't eating, why don't you take Jack-Jack out for a walk? I don't know what's gotten into the two of you," said Greg, Sr.

"Thanks, Dad," Junebug said with excited relief as he stared at the steaming pot on the table. "Ahh-nice to meet you, Mr. and Mrs. Rillieux. See-see-see you later." Junebug backed slowly from the room, forcing a big smile for the two guests.

Once out of the dining room, Junebug turned quickly and sprinted for the front door with Jack-Jack at his heels. He stopped once he was out on the porch.

"So that's what you were trying to tell me!" Junebug said to Jack-Jack as he kneeled down to rub his head. "That's right, boy! No gumbo for you and me! Not ever!"

ABOUT THE AUTHOR

A native of Live Oak, Florida, Tameka Bradley Hobbs is the author of *To Collect, Protect, and Serve: Behind the Scenes at the Library of Virginia*, published in 2011. Hobbs is married to author William Ashanti Hobbs, III, and together they are the proud parents of two sons, Ashanti and Amiri. The family currently lives in South Florida. She can be reached at junebug.gumbo.garden@gmail.com.

ABOUT THE ILLUSTRATOR

Jason Austin studied graphic design at County College of Morris in Randolph, NJ and later transferred to New Jersey City University, graduating with a bachelor's degree in Illustration in 2006. He has since worked as a professional graphic designer and freelance illustrator. Jason has also self-published his own comic book series titled, *The Cosmic Samaritan*. He currently lives in Northeastern New Jersey. Visit his website at http://jfastudios.carbonmade.com/.